GHANA:
A PLACE I CALL HOME

MONICA HABIA

Written by Monica Habia
Illustrated by Amakai Quaye
Designed by Reyhana Ismail

All inquiries or sales request should be addressed to:

PLANTING PEOPLE
GROWING JUSTICE

Planting People Growing Justice Press
P.O. Box 131894
Saint Paul, MN 55113
www.ppgjli.org

Printed and bound in the United States of America
First Edition

LCCN: 2020939781
ISBN: 978-0-9985553-6-2

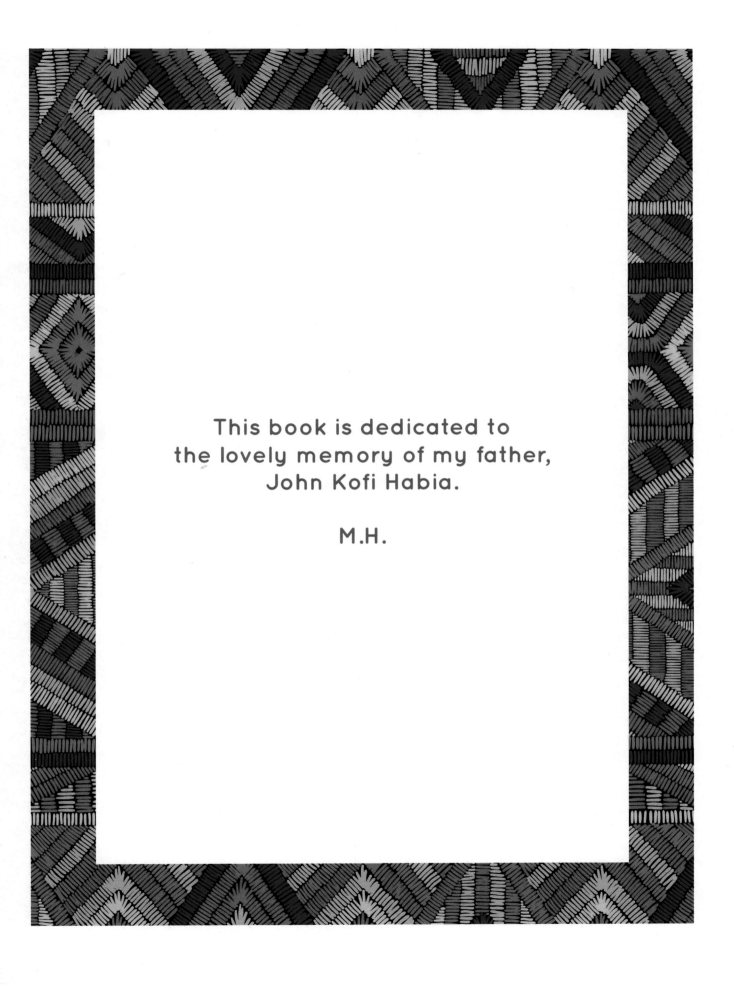

This book is dedicated to
the lovely memory of my father,
John Kofi Habia.

M.H.

Every afternoon, Grandpa would stand on the front steps anxiously waiting for Samuel to arrive home from school.

He shouted with joy, "Welcome home, Samuel! How was your school day?"

Samuel smiled brightly and joined Grandpa in the living room. He could not wait to talk about his day at school.

"Grandpa, our teacher asked us to learn more about who we are and where we came from. This is our history project. Can you please help me?" Samuel asked.

Grandpa beamed with pride and joy, then he said, "Of course, I have been waiting a long time to share with you about our home, Ghana. Grab a pencil and paper. Did you know this year is the Year of Return?"

Samuel shook his head and responded, "No, what does that mean?"

Grandpa explained, "Some 400 years ago, the first enslaved Africans were taken from their home and brought to the United States. The Year of Return is an invitation for all Africans abroad to return to Ghana and experience their lost heritage and identity."

Samuel loved to travel. He jumped to his feet and said, "Let's pack our bags and go!"

Grandpa chuckled and reminded Samuel about the special Ghana trip Grandma was planning for the family next year.

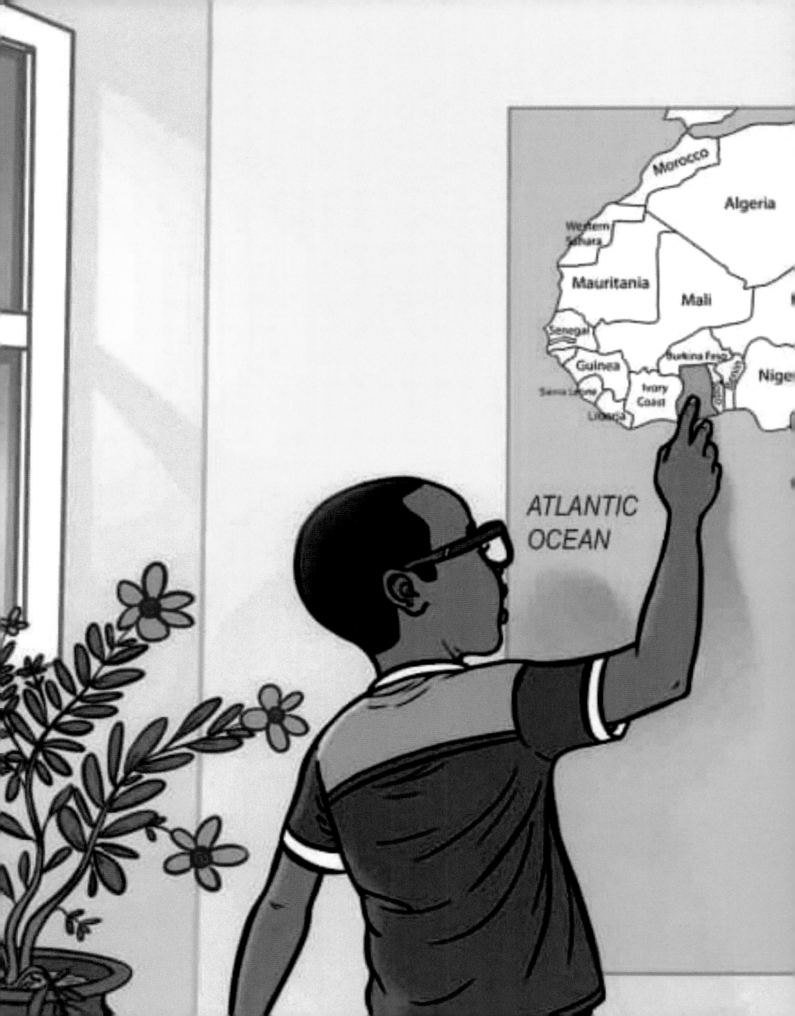

"Ghana is formerly known as the Gold Coast. It is one of the largest producers of gold in Africa," Grandpa said. The country lies on the west coast along the Atlantic Ocean. "Samuel, can you point out Ghana on the map of Africa?"

"Yes, the map of Africa is huge," Samuel responded and pointed to the west coast of Africa.

Grandpa beamed with pride and said, "Africa is the second-largest continent in the world with 54 countries. We call our home Mama Africa. Her claim to fame is being the Earth's oldest populated area. Civilization began in Africa."

Grandpa continued, "Accra, the capital city of Ghana, is a beautiful city. The weather is warm and sunny. It is truly paradise. The first sign you will see reads: AKWAABA, meaning 'welcome' in Twi. Twi is one of the many local languages spoken in Ghana."

"Akwaaba," Samuel repeated and extended his hands wide. Samuel gave Grandpa a hug.

"How many languages are in Ghana?" Samuel asked.

"There are many languages spoken. I speak five: Twi, Ewe, Ga, Fante, and Hausa. I will begin by teaching you how to count in each language," Grandpa replied.

"I remember our first breakfast," Grandpa said with a slight grin. "I still can taste the fluffy scrambled eggs, delicious beans and buttery toast. I finished my meal with hot cocoa."

"You are making me hungry," Samuel said while rubbing his stomach.

Grandpa shared, "Wait, I had another treat for my afternoon snack. I had the best chocolate bar. This is because Ghana is the world's second-largest cocoa-producing country. I will make sure you get a chocolate bar and I know you will love it."

"I can't wait," Samuel said. "You know I love chocolate, Grandpa."

"Our first visit will be at the Dr. W.E.B. DuBois Memorial Center," Grandpa continued. "The center was his home where he studied and wrote books. Did you know that Dr. DuBois lived in Ghana?"

"We learned about Dr. DuBois at school. He was a great writer, historian, and teacher. He worked on a special encyclopedia called: *Encyclopedia Africana*," Samuel replied. Grandpa smiled proudly as Samuel shared about Dr. DuBois.

DR KWAME NKRUMAH

MALCOM . X

"Now let me tell you about our second stop. It was at the Kwame Nkrumah Memorial Park and Museum. At the museum, you can see pictures of him with leaders such as President John F. Kennedy, Malcolm X, Muhammad Ali, and Rev. Dr. Martin Luther King, Jr."

"Who is he? I never heard his name before," Samuel asked.

Grandpa said, "Dr. Kwame Nkrumah loved our country and our people. He was a strong leader who had a vision of a united Africa. He became the first president of Ghana in 1957 after Ghana gained its independence."

"Grandma and I had fun at the beach," Grandpa said. Grandpa nodded his head and continued, "And we also enjoyed a horse ride, played beach ball, and collected some seashells."

Samuel then asked Grandpa, "Are those seashells on the dresser from Ghana?" Grandpa responded, "Yes, they are from the beautiful shores of the Atlantic Ocean."

Grandpa pointed and said to Samuel, "This huge white building is the Cape Coast Castle, one of about forty slave castles in Ghana. At the castle, we learned about how free African people were captured and sold off as slaves. We saw the dungeons where enslaved Africans stayed until they were shipped far from home and we also saw the famous 'Door of No Return'."

"What do you mean by 'Door of No Return'?" Samuel asked. "This was the last point our brothers and sisters saw before boarding the slave ship, never to return. Famous people from around the world, like United States President Barack Obama, have visited the castle to honor our ancestors," Grandpa said as he wiped tears from his eyes.

"It sounds like a sad place, but I want to go and learn more about our history. Can we go someday?" Samuel asked Grandpa. Grandpa gave Samuel a reassuring nod and said, "Yes, we sure will."

"On our last day, we went to the Art Market to buy gifts for friends and family. We exchanged our U.S. dollar for Ghanaian cedi," Grandpa said. Grandpa handed Samuel a few cedis. Grandpa chuckled and said to Samuel, "Your grandma spent all our cedis. She bought colorful Ankara fabric, Kente, earrings, necklace, bracelets, and beads."

"Now I know why Grandma likes to wear all these colorful clothes," Samuel said to Grandpa. "So, what did you get, Grandpa?"

Grandpa responded, "I bought paintings and carvings."

Grandpa looked at Samuel and said, "We did so many amazing things for our one-week stay in Ghana. We had a boat ride, made new friends, and learned how to dance. I have a lot to teach in our next family history session. Always remember, Ghana is a place I call home."

Samuel hugged Grandpa and said to him with excitement, "Ghana is a place I call home, too! I cannot wait to visit."

Overview of the Year of Return

2019 marked the 400th anniversary of the first enslaved Africans' arrival in the United States in 1619. This was a time to pause, reflect, and act. Momentum is building nationally and globally. In 2013, the UN declared 2015–2024 the International Decade for People of African Descent to "promote respect, protection and fulfilment of all human rights and fundamental freedoms of people of African descent." Furthermore, H.R.1242—400 Years of African-American History Commission Act—was passed on May 1, 2017, and established the Commission to develop and carry out activities throughout the United States to commemorate the 400th anniversary of the arrival of Africans in the English colonies at Point Comfort, Virginia, in 1619. Moreover, Ghana President Akufo-Addo declared a clarion call to take action by announcing 2019 as "The Year of Return."

The time is now for a Sankofa moment. Sankofa reflects the philosophy of "go back and fetch it." It also means "we must return to the source." Through a candid discussion about the legacy of slavery, we first must pay homage to the enslaved Africans who shaped the course of world history and advanced global development through their hard work, fierce determination, and unwavering faith. Their blood, sweat, and tears nourished the fertile soil of our global economies. As we experience a Sankofa moment, we will also discover our shared humanity and common destiny. This will challenge each of us to keep our hands on the plow by eradicating the injustices manifested in our laws and policies. Hold on, hold steadfast to the cause of justice and freedom for all!

Dr. Artika R. Tyner, Founder- Planting People Growing Justice Leadership Institute

Planting People Growing Justice Leadership Institute's 2019 Year of Return Trip

A special visit with His Royal Majesty- Odeneho Kwafo Akoto III - Akwamumanhene

Map of Africa

Map of Ghana

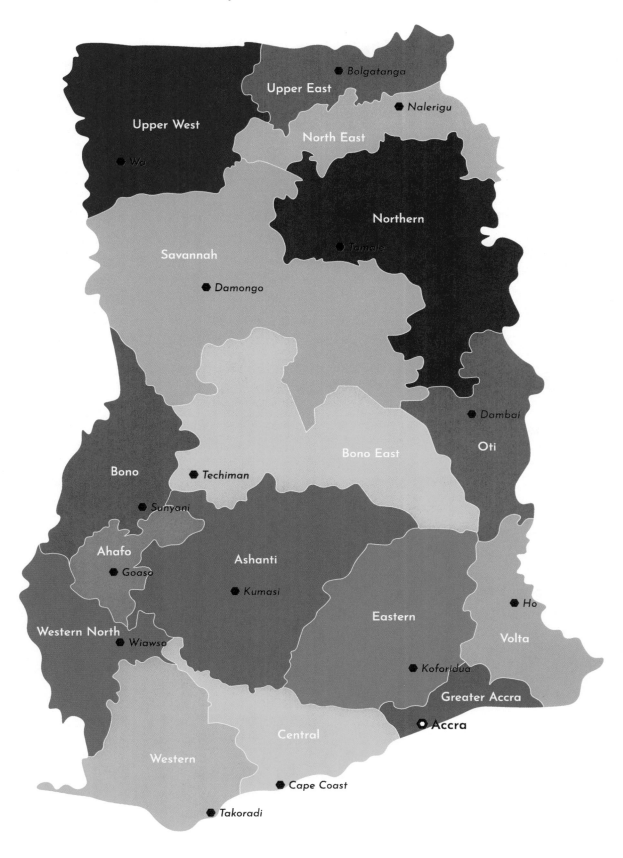

Flag of Ghana

The National flag was designed by Mrs. Theodosia Salome Okoh to replace the flag of the United Kingdom of Britain and Ireland upon the attainment of independence in 1957. The flag of Ghana consists of red, gold, and green colors in horizontal lines. A five-point black star is in the center of the gold stripe.

1. RED represents the blood of those who died in the country's struggle for independence
2. GOLD represents the mineral wealth of the country
3. GREEN symbolizes the country's rich forest and
4. THE BLACK STAR stands for the lodestar of African freedom

Source: Ghanaweb.com

National Pledge

I promise, on my honor
To be faithful and loyal to Ghana
my motherland,
I pledge myself to the service of
Ghana with all my strength
and with all my heart,
I promise to hold in high esteem
our heritage, won for us
through the blood and toil
of our fathers,
And I pledge myself to uphold
and defend the good name
of Ghana.
So help me God.

Source: Ghana Nation, ghananation.com/content/article/92-the-national-anthem-and-pledge.html

National Anthem

1. God bless our homeland Ghana
And make our nation great and strong,
Bold to defend forever
The cause of Freedom and of Right,
Fill our hearts with true humility,
Make us cherish fearless honesty,
And help us to resist oppressors' rule
With all our will and might forever more.

2. Hail to the name, O Ghana,
To thee we make our solemn vow;
Steadfast to build together
A nation strong in Unity,
With our gifts of mind and strength of arm,
Whether night or day, in mist or storm,
In every need whate'er the call may be
To serve thee, Ghana, now and ever more.

3. Raise high the flag of Ghana,
And one with Africa advance,
Black Star of hope and honor
To all who thirst for liberty.
Where the banner of Ghana freely flies,
May the way to freedom truly lie,
Arise, arise, O sons of Ghanaland,
And under God march on forever more.

Glossary

Abroad: A foreign country.

Cedi: The currency of Ghana.

Encyclopedia Africana: A book written by Dr. W.E.B. DuBois that tells the story and experiences of Africans and African Americans.

Enslaved Africans: Persons from Africa who were forced to work for no pay, to obey commands, and lose their freedom.

Kente: A type of silk and cotton fabric made of interwoven cloth strips. It is native to the Akan ethnic group of Ghana.

About the Author
Monica Yaa Habia

Monica Yaa Habia was born and raised in Ghana. She believes in the power of quality education and is committed to bridging the knowledge gap of Africa through her writings and research. She currently lives in Minnesota and is a program design and support professional for organizations including non-profits and educational institutions.

About the Illustrator
Amakai Quaye

Amakai Quaye is a dynamic contemporary artist, from Ghana. As an artist, Amakai is an impressionist, whose paintings consists of vibrant colors, movements, expressions, and textures which he freely executes with witty palette knife strokes. With his background as an illustrator, his artworks are mostly figurative, with themes bordering around Jazz music, fashion, and everyday life. He also paints abstracts, portraits, and landscapes.

About Planting People Growing Justice Leadership Institute

Planting People Growing Justice Leadership Institute seeks to plant seeds of social change through education, training, and community outreach.

A portion of proceeds from this book will support the educational programming of Planting People Growing Justice Leadership Institute.

Learn more at www.ppgjli.org

Made in the USA
Monee, IL
05 November 2020